DAT

BEECHWOOD BUNNY TALES

POPPY'S DANCE

For a free color catalog describing Gareth Stevens' list of
high-quality children's books, call 1-800-341-3569 (USA)
or 1-800-461-9120 (Canada).

Beechwood Bunny Tales
Dandelion's Vanishing Vegetable Garden
Mistletoe and the Baobab Tree
Periwinkle at the Full Moon Ball
Poppy's Dance

Library of Congress Cataloging-in-Publication Data

Huriet, Geneviève.
    [Danse de Romarin Passiflore. English]
    Poppy's dance / illustrated by Loïc Jouannigot ; written by Geneviève Huriet ;
[English text by MaryLee Knowlton].
        p. cm. — (Beechwood bunny tales)
    Translation of: La danse de Romarin Passiflore.
    Summary: Precocious Poppy takes a risk when he ventures in the snow to find
some cabbage for his family.
    ISBN 0-8368-0528-3
    [1. Rabbits—Fiction.] I. Jouannigot, Loïc, ill. II. Title. III. Series.
PZ7.H95657Po   1991   [E]—dc20   90-46858

North American edition first published in 1991 by
Gareth Stevens Children's Books
1555 North RiverCenter Drive, Suite 201
Milwaukee, Wisconsin 53212, USA

English text by MaryLee Knowlton

Printed in the United States of America

1 2 3 4 5 6 7 8 9 95 94 93 92 91

BEECHWOOD BUNNY TALES

POPPY'S DANCE

written by GENEVIÈVE HURIET   illustrated by LOÏC JOUANNIGOT

Gareth Stevens Children's Books
MILWAUKEE

No one in the Bellflower bunny family — or in Beechwood Grove — could remember such a winter. A harsh wind had swept in from the north. The creek had been frozen for weeks, and the trees bowed under the snow, which was falling thick and fast.

6

From inside the house, Periwinkle, Poppy, Dandelion, Violette, and Mistletoe watched the snow swirl outside. "I knew we were in for an awful winter when all the storks flew south in August," Poppy sighed sadly.

"Well, at least we have plenty to eat," Violette suggested hopefully. "We have carrots, turnips, apples, potatoes, pumpkins, and — best of all — pickled, canned, and dried cabbages."

Mistletoe, Periwinkle, and Dandelion were cheered by the thought — especially the part about the cabbages.

But not Poppy.

"We don't have any fresh cabbage leaves," he complained. "That's what I like best."

Now his brothers were gloomy, too.

"Pull yourselves together, boys," Violette scolded. "Let's draw pictures of cabbages and decorate the house with them."

Soon all the Bellflower bunnies were busy — except for Poppy. Nothing could make him forget fresh cabbage leaves.

"You can have your play cabbages," he announced grumpily. "I'm going to find real ones."

11

As fast as he could throw a scarf around his neck, Poppy bounded out into the snow. Through the village he ran, hither and yon, to and fro, searching the most sheltered gardens for a cabbage that might have escaped the freeze. He found not so much as a leaf.

Poppy's paws were soon numb and his tail was stiff. He ducked into a deserted burrow to warm himself.

In no hurry to go back out into the cold, he decided to explore. He crawled to the end of a long, dry tunnel and poked his head out. Much to his surprise, he found himself in the midst of the strangest band of rabbits he had ever seen.

These rabbits were white and so fat that they seemed unable to move. As Poppy crawled out of the tunnel, they wrinkled their noses and said nothing.

The silence made Poppy uneasy. He struggled to his feet, brushed himself off, and bowed. "Poppy Bellflower at your service," he said.

"Cornelius Angora," an enormous rabbit replied solemnly.

"My, how you fidget!" exclaimed one lady rabbit in a snooty voice. "Are you cold?"

"Oh, I'm not cold," Poppy replied. He wasn't admitting anything to this unfriendly group. "Nice weather for a dance, don't you think?"

And with that, he began to jump in place.

"Ah, yes," laughed the lady rabbit. "You country bunnies do like to move about, don't you? Hollowing tunnels, gardening, dancing . . . such quaint customs."

Poppy knew a snooty remark when he heard one.

"I'll show them how 'country bunnies' act!" he decided. He stopped jumping and moved into a dance. The frozen ground echoed under his prancing paws as he sashayed forward and back, sliding and crossing. He cut capers, did a jig, and moved on to tap dancing, clip tig-adi, clap tig-ada. Finally, he ended — breathlessly — with a perfect leap.

"Bravo! Bravo, Poppy! Encore!" The applause and cheers rang through the frozen air. The younger rabbits began to waddle heavily, trying to imitate Poppy's dance.

Cornelius Angora seemed troubled by the chaos around him. Pulling cabbage leaves from beneath his robe, he wrapped Poppy's muffler around them. "It seems you have become a star with our children, Poppy," he said. "I think you had better go before they forget everything we've taught them."

The sounds of applause and cheers followed Poppy through the tunnel as he headed for home. He held the cabbage close to his heart and thought proudly of the entrance he would make at home: a star!

"Poppy! Where have you been?" asked Violette worriedly.

"I've been to get cabbage leaves, just as I promised," Poppy replied. "All I had to do was dance! And they liked my dancing so much that they gave me cabbage leaves."

"Who gave you these cabbage leaves?" demanded Violette.

"The biggest, whitest rabbits you've ever seen!" replied Poppy gleefully. "They couldn't even dance!"

"Poppy! You silly rabbit!" Violette cried in horror. "You were in a rabbit pen! Those rabbits are being raised for someone's dinner. You could have been put in a stew if you had been caught."

Violette was so upset that she began to cry. Poppy bowed his head in shame. How foolish and vain he had been!

"What's the trouble here?" It was Papa Bramble.

Poppy threw a pleading look at Violette. "Poppy found cabbage leaves, Papa," she said.

"Why, Poppy! How did you do that?" asked his pleased father.

Quickly, Violette continued. "He danced for some rabbits, and they gave him the cabbage as a gift," she said smoothly. "Now let's go in. I'm cold."

Papa Bramble stared after them, scratching his chin. He wondered if he would ever understand his children.

In the house, everyone admired Periwinkle's clay brussels sprouts, Violette's cabbage necklace, and Mistletoe's orange Chinese cabbages. They cheered when Dandelion came through the door carrying the creamed canned cabbages that he and Aunt Zinnia had cooked.

But when Poppy showed them his fresh, crisp cabbage leaves, the house shook with noisy joy!

What a feast they had that night! After dinner, they sat around the fire and chatted contentedly.

"Poppy, when will you dance again for the rabbits who gave you the cabbage?" asked Mistletoe, already hungry for more.

Poppy hesitated, remembering the applause and the shouts of "Bravo!" and "Encore!" But then he glanced at Violette, and she gave him a sharp look.

"I think once was enough," he replied. "Once was plenty, indeed."